PRIN
PRANCES
AGAIN

Heather Grovet

Pacific Press® Publishing Association
Nampa, Idaho
Oshawa, Ontario, Canada

Edited by Jerry D. Thomas
Designed by Dennis Ferree
Cover art by Mary Rumford
Inside art by Mary Rumford

Library of Congress Cataloging-in-Publication Data

Grovet, Heather, 1963-
    Prince prances again/Heather Grovet.
        p. cm.—(Julius and friends; bk.9)
    Summary: Janelle is happy to finally have a pony
of her own, but when her new friend Katie almost
ruins her summer, Janelle must pray hard to Jesus
before she can forgive Katie.
    ISBN 0-8163-1807-7
    [1. Ponies. 2. Forgiveness. 3. Friendship. 4. Chris-
tian life.] I. Title. II. Series.

PZ7.G931825 Pr 2001
—dc21   00-062398

01 02 03 04 05 • 5 4 3 2 1

Contents

Other Books in the Julius and Friends Series

Dedication

*To my husband, Doug and
our own little pony lovers:
Danelle and Kaitlin*

CHAPTER

1

A Wild Pony Ride!

The warm sunshine, the smell of flowers in the air, the never-ending singing of the birds—it could all only mean one thing: winter was finally over and spring had arrived. And with the new spring came something Janelle had wanted for a long time—a summer with her very own horse, Prince.

But Janelle had a worried frown on her face as she stood by the fence with her father. "You're going to hurt Prince!" she said.

Her father smiled and patted the black pony on the shoulder. "It's not going to hurt this fellow to have me ride him a mile or two," he said.

"But he's too little," Janelle said. She studied Prince carefully. Although it was the end of April, the pony still had a full coat of winter hair. His mane had grown several inches and covered his neck like a bushy black mop. Only a corner of the white star on his forehead peeked through his heavy forelock.

"Are you sure you won't hurt him?" Janelle asked.

"Prince is a Welsh pony," Mr. Wilson said. "He may be little, but he's tough. Back in Wales, these ponies used to work underground in the coal mines hauling heavy loads of coal." Mr. Wilson smiled at his daughter. "He's like you—small but mighty!"

Janelle flipped her own black ponytail of hair impatiently. "But why can't I ride him first?"

Mr. Wilson slipped the reins over the pony's neck. "Look, Prince is fat and full of energy—and he hasn't been ridden all winter. It wouldn't surprise me if he bucks a few times."

"Prince doesn't buck," Janelle said.

"I guess we'll see, won't we?" Mr. Wilson replied.

He felt the pony's cinch, and then frowned. "Still up to your tricks of puffing up your belly, hey?" Mr. Wilson asked. Mr. Wilson pulled the cinch tightly, shortening it another inch or so. "Well, I want it snug today."

Prince pinned his ears back, but didn't move.

"That's too tight, Daddy," Janelle fretted.

"Sorry, Prince," Mr. Wilson said, patting the pony. "But we have to be safe. Now, let's see if I can still get on a horse."

Janelle almost giggled as she watched her father try to fit his large boot into the small stirrup of the child's size saddle. Prince watched him warily out of one eye. Even with the saddle tight it still tipped to one side as Mr. Wilson hauled himself into place. Mr. Wilson leaned his weight hard onto the other stirrup, pulling the saddle straight.

Now Janelle laughed out loud. "Oh, Dad, you look so funny!"

Mr. Wilson's long legs were pulled up unnaturally high as he tried to make them fit in the short stirrups. His tall body seemed to tower over the black pony's head. Prince's ears flicked back and forth, and he snorted a time or two.

"All right, buddy," Mr. Wilson said, pulling his cowboy hat down firmly on his head. "Let's see if you can behave yourself."

For a moment Prince didn't move. Mr. Wilson brought his heels down firmly on the pony's round sides.

Janelle saw a streak of black as the pony suddenly bolted across the yard.

"Whoa!" Mr. Wilson yelled. The pony tore forward, scattering mud, and then planted his front feet. As Janelle watched Prince began to buck. The pony squealed—there were several hard leaps—and Mr. Wilson's hat flew from his head and landed near a puddle.

"Whoa, there!" Mr. Wilson bellowed. Janelle could see inches of air between her father's backside and the saddle as the pony bounced sideways. The hat disappeared under one black hoof and in a moment reappeared, muddy and squashed.

"My hat!" Mr. Wilson yelled. He pulled on one rein, turning the pony around in a small circle. Prince spun past the hat, narrowly missing it a second time, and then dashed down the lane.

"Are you OK, Daddy?" Janelle called.

Her father raised one hand but didn't turn around. In a few seconds the pair disappeared out of sight behind some trees. Janelle walked over to the cowboy hat, and gingerly picked it up. What a muddy mess.

"Dad's going to be mad about his hat," Janelle said to herself. She sighed, and walked over to the tack shed. She sat down on a log, and waited for her father and Prince to return.

Dear Jesus, Janelle prayed, closing her eyes for a moment. *Please help Prince be good for Dad. And don't let Dad get bucked off.* As she listened a bird began to warble a song in the trees nearby. Janelle took a deep breath, smelling the spring air. *And please, don't let Dad get too mad at Prince.*

In about twenty minutes, Prince and Mr. Wilson returned. Prince's long hair was damp with sweat, and he was walking quietly now. When they stopped in front of Janelle Mr. Wilson slid clumsily off the pony. He groaned, and rubbed his back.

"I should be down kissing the ground," Mr. Wilson said. He straightened his back slowly. "Next year I'll put you on first!"

"Did you fall off?" Janelle asked.

"No," Mr. Wilson groaned. "But I feel like

I was trampled by a herd of ponies!"

"Sorry, Daddy," Janelle said. She gave Prince a stern look. Prince swished his tail cheerfully.

"Where's my hat?" Mr. Wilson asked.

Janelle slowly held the cowboy hat out. Mr. Wilson moaned again.

"Do you have any idea how much that hat cost?" he asked, glaring at Prince.

Janelle thought for a moment that the pony smiled. But of course that was silly—ponies couldn't smile—could they? "I'm sorry Prince was so bad," she said.

Mr. Wilson sighed and handed Janelle the reins. "Janelle, this is just part of horse ownership. Horses can be silly in the spring. And Prince has been overfed and under-worked."

"You aren't going to sell him, are you?" Janelle asked, holding her breath.

"Do you think I should?" Mr. Wilson asked.

Janelle shook her head quickly.

"We're not going to sell Prince," Mr. Wilson said. "But we've got our work cut out for us. Now, unsaddle your pony and give him a good rub-down."

"Sure," Janelle said. She began to un-buckle the saddle.

"Then we need to make some plans," Mr. Wilson continued. "No more grain for this fellow. He needs to lose some weight. That will make him less foolish."

"He is a bit fat, isn't he?" Janelle said. She took a stiff brush, and began to work it through the sweaty hair on Prince's back. The pony dropped his head and stood quietly.

"Fat?" Mr. Wilson said. "You could play a board game on his back and the cards wouldn't fall off! Yes, he needs to lose some weight. And I can see I'll be doing a bit of riding this week."

"Sorry, Daddy," she said again.

Mr. Wilson grinned and ruffled Janelle's hair. "Don't worry," he said. "You're going to be busy, too."

"Busy?"

"That's right," Mr. Wilson said. "A certain little pony needs his hooves trimmed. And we have some fence that needs repairs. You look like just the person to help me."

Janelle nodded.

"I'll be back in a few minutes," Mr. Wilson said, dusting off the back of his pants. "When you're finished brushing Prince, please put the saddle away."

"OK, Daddy," Janelle agreed.

When Mr. Wilson left, Janelle threw her arms around the pony and gave his neck a squeeze. Prince opened his eyes briefly.

"You'd better behave yourself, Princey boy," Janelle said softly. "We're going to have the best summer ever. Because now you're my pony to keep."

PRINCE

CHAPTER
2

Katie Comes
for a Visit

"He's behaving a lot better today, isn't he?" Janelle asked. Mr. Wilson halted the pony near the tack shed and slid off his back.

"Yes, he's been a good boy," her father said. He patted the pony on the rump. Prince ignored Mr. Wilson as usual, and stretched his neck towards Janelle.

"Can I give him some oats, Daddy?" Janelle asked, rubbing the star on Prince's forehead.

"Give him a handful," Mr. Wilson said. "But he doesn't need more than that."

Janelle hopped into the tack shed and returned with both her hands cupped together, carrying a scoop of grain. Prince nickered softly.

"You're a little pig, aren't you?" Janelle teased, allowing the pony to eat the grain. She was careful to keep her fingers straight so they didn't get into Prince's mouth where he could accidentally bite her. When the grain was gone Prince rubbed against Janelle, asking for more.

"That's all, Princey boy," Janelle said.

"Do you want a ride before we unsaddle him?" Mr. Wilson asked.

"Uhhhh," Janelle hesitated. "Are you sure he won't buck?"

Mr. Wilson shook his head. "I'm not sure, but Prince has been well behaved the last few times I've ridden him. He's not a mean pony, you know. He just had too much energy."

Janelle remembered all the jumping and bucking that had happened earlier that week. She didn't want Prince to behave like that when she was riding!

Mr. Wilson seemed to know what she was thinking. "Here, put on your riding helmet, and I'll lead you around for a few minutes. I think you'll see that Prince isn't so frisky anymore."

Prince walked calmly behind Mr. Wilson. Finally Janelle nodded at her father. "OK, Dad," she said. "Let me ride alone now."

Mr. Wilson stepped back and watched as Janelle guided Prince around the small yard. She made him move in circles, first at a walk, and then at a trot.

"He's being good," Janelle called. She squeezed the pony's sides, and started him trotting down the lane. There was a wet, sticky sound as the pony's hooves clip-clopped on the muddy road and overhead a flock of Canada geese honked as they flew in their traditional V-formation.

"Hey, Janelle," Mr. Wilson suddenly yelled. "Quick, hang on tight!"

Janelle turned in the saddle to look at her father. "Why? What's the matter, Dad?"

"Birds!" Mr. Wilson exclaimed, pointing at the geese flying high overhead. "There's some of those nasty killer birds that Prince is so scared of!"

"Daddy!"

Mr. Wilson's booming laugh carried down the lane. Janelle pretended to ignore her father's teasing. She knew he was re-membering the time last year when Prince had startled some birds at his feet. When the birds flew up, Prince was frightened and ran away.

"That wasn't your fault, was it, Princey boy?" Janelle asked. She started to sing as they rode down the narrow lane. "I am so glad that Jesus loves me," Janelle sang. Her voice rose and fell with every step they took. "Jesus loves me—Jesus loves me—I am so glad that Jesus loves me—Jesus loves even me."

Janelle had just finished brushing Prince when an unfamiliar car pulled up by their house. As Janelle watched, a man and a girl got out of the car.

"Hello," Mr. Wilson called.

"Hi," the man replied. The pair walked towards Janelle. "My name's Gordon Adolph," the man said, holding out his hand to Janelle's father. "And this is my oldest daughter, Katie."

Janelle and Katie looked at each other. They were about the same size, and both girls wore their hair in high ponytails. But while Janelle's hair was black, Katie had light brown hair.

"How do you do?" Mr. Wilson said, shaking the man's hand.

"We just moved into the Cooper house

down the road," the man continued. "I hope you don't mind us stopping, but as we drove by we saw someone riding a horse and Katie begged me to stop. Katie's horse-crazy, aren't you, honey?"

Janelle looked at Katie. The girl nodded and smiled shyly. "Is that your pony?" she asked.

Janelle nodded. "This is Prince," she said, scratching the pony on the neck.

"Can I pet him?" Katie asked. Her bangs were too long, and she flipped them out of her eyes.

"Sure you can," Janelle said. "Prince likes kids."

Katie reached out her arm, and began to rub the pony's shoulder. Prince nuzzled the girl's hand for a moment, and then stood quietly.

"He's so sweet," Katie said.

Mr. Wilson turned to Katie's father. "Now, Gordon, why don't you come into the house and meet my wife. The girls can put Prince away and get to know each other."

"Well, that would be nice," Mr. Adolph said. "But we can only stay for a few minutes."

"Can I have a ride?" Katie asked.

"I could lead her, Daddy," Janelle said quickly.

Mr. Wilson turned to look at the other man. "Is it all right with you?" he asked.

Mr. Adolph nodded.

Janelle's father gave Katie a boost up onto Prince's wide back. "Hang onto his mane," Mr. Wilson instructed.

Katie took a firm grip of black hair. Janelle lead the pony around the yard several times, and then took him over to the corral. Katie slid off at the corral, and Janelle lead Prince inside the pen. Janelle took off the pony's halter, and shut the gate carefully behind her.

The two girls climbed up on the fence and looked at the pony. As they watched, Prince walked forward a few steps and began to paw at the ground with one hoof.

"No, Prince," Janelle called. "Don't do it!"

"What's the matter?" Katie asked.

"He's going to roll and get himself all muddy!"

As they watched the pony's feet buckled under him. He flopped over on one side, and began to roll on the wet ground.

"Prince!" Janelle yelled, but Prince didn't

look up. He rolled back and forth several times, and then got to his feet, shook himself, and lay down on his other side.

Janelle groaned. "Look at you," she scolded. "You're a big mess. And after all the work I did brushing you!"

When Prince got to his feet he seemed pleased with himself. Mud covered his sides, his back, and even his neck. His mane was plastered with mud and bits of straw. He shook himself merrily.

"Why did he do that?" Katie asked, trying not to laugh.

"Horses like to roll after a ride," Janelle explained. "My dad says it's the way they scratch their backs."

"You're so lucky," Katie said. "I wish I had a pony of my own."

"Maybe you can come over and visit us," Janelle said.

"That would be great," Katie said, with a big smile. "Hey, how old are you?"

"I'm ten," Janelle replied.

"Me, too! That means we'll be in the same grade at school!"

"I don't go to public school," Janelle said, climbing off the wooden rails. "I go to a little Christian school near Sedgewick."

"That's too bad," Katie said. She was still watching the pony. "Do you think I can still come over to visit you and Prince?"

"Sure," Janelle said happily. This *was* going to be a great year. A pony of her own, and a new friend who lived nearby!

CHAPTER
3

Prince and the Potato

"I think I've got everything ready," Janelle called to her parents. She studied the heap of equipment in the back of the truck. There was Prince's saddle, blanket, and bridle. The tack box held several different brushes and a hoof pick. A pail of grain, a container of bug spray, and an extra lead rope lay nearby.

"I wish you'd have taken up a lighter sport," Mr. Wilson grumbled, as he set Janelle's cowboy boots and riding helmet in the half-ton's back seat. "Like soccer. What does a soccer player need anyhow? A soccer ball and some shin pads!"

Janelle giggled.

"But, no," Mr. Wilson continued, winking

at his daughter. "You have to like horses!"

Mrs. Wilson shook her head. "Now, dear, weren't you the one who started all this?"

"Me! I think you have me mistaken for someone else," Mr. Wilson said, with a laugh. "Anyhow, let's load up Prince and get this show on the road."

They were just swinging the heavy trailer door shut when Katie and her father pulled up.

"Sorry I'm late," Katie called.

"I was afraid you weren't going to come," Janelle said. She held the truck door open for her friend.

"And miss 4-H!" Katie said. "No way!"

Mr. Adolph waved from the car. Two little girls in the car's back seat also waved, their faces pressed eagerly against the window.

"My little sisters wanted to come, too," Katie said, waving back.

"Do up your seatbelts," Mrs. Wilson instructed. In a moment the truck and horse trailer drove down the lane.

Janelle and Katie talked about horses all the way to town. Katie had been eagerly looking forward to the chance to see Janelle at her riding class.

"Do you think I could have a turn riding?"

Katie asked, as they pulled up at the arena.

Mr. Wilson turned around in his seat. "No, Katie," he said. "4-H rules say that nonmembers cannot ride during class."

"Why not?" Katie asked, frowning.

"It's for safety reasons," Mr. Wilson said. "Besides, Prince doesn't like 4-H very much. Even Janelle has problems making him cooperate."

"Maybe he'll be good this year," Janelle said.

Mr. Wilson rolled his eyes. "I'll have to see it to believe it."

Once Prince was unloaded Janelle tied him to the trailer, and then began to brush him. "I am so glad that Jesus loves me," Janelle began to sing, smiling at her friend. "Jesus loves even me."

Katie frowned at Janelle.

Janelle stopped her song. *What's her problem?* she thought. *I'm not that terrible of a singer! Maybe she just doesn't like Christian songs.* Janelle didn't sing anymore.

Prince wasn't pleased about being at 4-H. He wouldn't walk in circles with the other horses until Janelle swatted him with the crop, and even then he tried to stop twice, causing other horses to bump into him. By the time the class was finished, Janelle's face was flushed and her legs were tired from squeezing so hard.

"You make me so mad sometimes," Janelle muttered.

Prince flicked his tail impatiently. *You make me mad too* he seemed to be saying.

"We're going to play a game today," the 4-H leader announced. Two adults began to roll several large barrels into the arena. The children watched with interest as he explained what they would be doing.

"This is called the potato race," the man continued. "It's a fun game, and it helps teach turning and stopping control." He pointed to the first barrel. "Each barrel will have three potatoes on it. You are to ride to the barrel, pick up one potato, hurry down to the tire at the other end of the arena, and drop the potato in the tire."

Someone giggled, and the leader paused until it was quiet. "Now," he said. "If the potato doesn't land inside the center of the tire, you need to dismount from your horse, pick up the potato and mount again. You can't go on until your potato lands inside the hole. Then you rush back to the barrel and get the next potato."

A boy on a gray horse held up his hand. "How many potatoes are there?" he asked.

"Each person will have three potatoes," the leader repeated. "Now, two kids will go at a time. Who would like to be first?"

Janelle watched with interest as two older boys lined their horses up at one end of the arena. At the leader's signal they galloped towards the first barrel, each boy trying to grab a potato quickly. One of the horses was frightened of the barrel and wouldn't walk close to it.

Janelle patted Prince's shoulder. "We can do this, Princey boy," she whispered. "If you'll just cooperate."

Before long Janelle and Prince stood in line. Across from them was a girl on a much larger brown horse.

"You can do it, Prince!" Katie yelled from the sidelines.

Janelle waved back.

"On your marks—get set—go!" the leader called.

Prince wouldn't move until Janelle swatted him with the crop. Then he trotted slowly but calmly over to the first barrel. Janelle was able to easily lean over and grab a potato. They trotted across the arena and stopped beside the tire. Prince watched with interest as Janelle leaned over and carefully aimed the potato at the hole in the center of the tire. *Plop*—it landed in the hole.

Janelle spun Prince around, and urged him back to the barrel for her second potato. Glancing over, Janelle noticed they were just ahead of the girl on the brown horse.

This time Prince sniffed the potatoes as Janelle scooped one up. "Come on, Princey boy," she hissed, kicking him firmly. Prince laid his ears back, but trotted down the arena to the tire again.

When they returned to the barrel for the third potato Prince again reached his nose over to smell the potato. "Watch out, Prince," Janelle ordered, trying to reach for the vegetable. Prince sniffed once again and then before Janelle could stop him he opened his mouth. There was a loud *crunch* as the pony took a bite out of the potato.

"PRINCE!" Janelle screeched. The pony jumped, and dropped the remaining half of the potato on the ground. Janelle looked around, uncertain what to do.

People began to laugh and point their direction.

"Pick up the potato," the leader called to Janelle.

She hesitated and then jumped off Prince. Picking up the slightly munched potato, she climbed back into the saddle, and trotted Prince down the end of the arena again. The girl with the big brown horse was finished before Janelle had even dropped the last potato in the tire.

Katie helped Janelle brush Prince before they loaded him in the trailer. "Prince is so funny," Katie said. She scratched the pony's neck.

"He's a brat!" Janelle replied with a smile. "But I love him anyhow."

Love's a funny thing, Janelle thought to herself. *I love Prince, even though he's not a perfect pony.* She remembered what Pastor Johnson had talked about at school worship. *Jesus loves us even when we're unkind and unlovable. Sometimes I think I can understand how Jesus feels.*

Janelle thought about sharing her ideas with Katie, and then she hesitated. If Katie didn't like her song, she probably wouldn't like to hear about Jesus either.

I don't think Katie likes Christian stuff, Janelle finally decided. *Maybe I'll tell her another day.*

PRINCE

CHAPTER

4

Katie is a Pest

"Look what I got!" Katie said, rushing into the Wilson house. The girl held up a large shoebox.

"What is it?" Janelle asked.

"Cowboy boots!" Katie exclaimed. "Dad said that I needed safe boots when I ride Prince. And look—they're real leather!"

Mr. Adolph smiled at Janelle's parents. "Thanks for letting Katie visit again." He lowered his voice, but Janelle could still catch his words. "She hasn't had a very good week."

"Come and look!" Katie called again. Janelle followed the girl into the front room slowly. She knew she shouldn't be eavesdropping on the adult's conversation, but she was curious.

She could still hear Mr. Adolph, ". . . she's been crying," he was saying. There was a moment when his voice dropped, and then he spoke slightly louder, ". . . I know she really misses her mother. The only time she seems happy is when she's here playing with Janelle. And your pony, of course."

Janelle's father patted the man on the shoulder. "We're glad to have her," he said.

Janelle thought about that conversation as she admired Katie's boots. *Where is Katie's mom?* she thought. Janelle hadn't met Mrs. Adolph, but she hadn't really thought about it. *Had she died? Or moved away? And if so, why hadn't Katie said anything about it?*

"Let's go get Prince," Katie said eagerly.

We don't talk about anything except horses, Janelle thought. But she smiled at her new friend, and hurried down to her room to get her own cowboy boots.

Mr. Wilson came outside and watched as the two girls caught Prince. "You brush one side and I'll brush the other," Katie ordered, picking up a horse brush.

"OK," Janelle said. Prince stood quietly as the two girls cleaned him.

"He's sure getting shiny," Katie said, admiring the sleek black pony.

"His winter hair's almost all gone," Janelle agreed. She tried to smooth down Prince's mane, but one clump insisted on standing upright.

The girls saddled Prince, and then Mr. Wilson put the pony's bridle on. "Who's going first?" he asked, slipping the reins over Prince's neck.

"Me!" Katie called.

Janelle raised her eyebrows, but didn't say anything. *Prince is my pony,* she thought. *I should be able to ride first.* Sometimes she wished Katie didn't like horses quite as much as she did.

Mr. Wilson showed the girl how to put her foot in the stirrup and get into the saddle. "I'm glad you have cowboy boots," Mr. Wilson said, smiling at Katie. "It's important that everyone rides with a heel. That way your foot can't slide through the stirrup and get stuck."

"These were pretty expensive," Katie said. She looked down at her feet admiringly. "My little sisters wanted some, too, but Dad said No."

Janelle looked at her own boots. They were a year old now, and slightly scuffed and dirty from use. She felt a twinge of jealousy. *Katie sure is being a show-off today,* she thought.

As Janelle watched, Mr. Wilson showed Katie how to hold the reins in her hands. "When you want to turn to the right," Mr. Wilson said, "you pull gently with your right hand. As soon as Prince begins to turn, you quit pulling. That's his reward for listening to you."

Mr. Wilson explained how to stop, and start, and turn the pony. Then he walked beside Katie as she guided Prince forward. Janelle sifted her weight impatiently, watching the pair.

"Let loose on the reins," Mr. Wilson instructed. "Remember, when Prince stops, you quit pulling. That's how he knows he did the right thing."

Janelle sighed and sat down on a pile of boards. This was very boring. *What I really want to do is take Prince out for a ride in the field,* Janelle thought. *That's a lot more fun than this.*

"Is it my turn now?" Janelle called.

Mr. Wilson raised his hand but didn't look her way. "In a few minutes," he said.

It seemed to take a lot more than a few minutes before Katie got off the black pony. Janelle mounted and waited while her father shortened the stirrups a bit.

"My legs are longer than yours," Katie said.

Janelle nodded but didn't reply.

"OK," Mr. Wilson said. "You're all set."

"I'm going to ride down the lane and around the granaries," Janelle said. "All right?"

"That'll be fine," Mr. Wilson said. "I'm going over to the garage to work on the lawn mower. Call me when you get back."

"Can I come with you?" Katie asked Janelle.

"What do you mean?" Janelle asked, nudging Prince into a walk.

"I'll walk beside you," Katie said. She began to walk by Prince's shoulder, and even reached out to pat the pony as they were moving.

Janelle hesitated. "I guess so," she finally said.

It didn't work very well. Katie talked

nonstop and bounced from one side of the lane to the other, sometimes getting in Prince's way. And when Janelle started to trot the pony, Katie ran beside them for a moment and then began to complain.

"Slow down," Katie called. "I can't keep up."

"I want to trot a bit farther," Janelle said.

"You have to walk," Katie said, panting. "I'm getting tired."

Janelle sighed, but brought Prince back to a walk. She knew she shouldn't be feeling so impatient with Katie, but she couldn't help herself. Maybe having a horse-riding friend wasn't going to be that much fun after all.

At bedtime that evening, Mrs. Wilson read a chapter from a book aloud to Janelle. Then they turned off the light, and Mrs. Wilson sat on the edge of Janelle's bed to talk.

"Did you have a good visit with Katie?" Mrs. Wilson asked.

Janelle hesitated. "Well," she said. "I guess so."

"You guess so?"

Janelle sighed. "Mom, does Katie have to come over so often?"

Mrs. Wilson looked puzzled. "I thought you two were friends. Did you have a fight today?"

"No," Janelle said. "But she has been so bossy lately. She thinks that she owns Prince. Why, today she told me that Prince likes her better than me! And that's not true!"

"Oh, dear." Mrs. Wilson began to rub Janelle's back. "Why do you think Katie's acting like that?"

"I don't know," Janelle said impatiently. "And I don't care. If she can't act nice, than I don't want her coming over to play."

Mrs. Wilson thought for a moment, and then finally spoke. "Janelle, Katie's having a lot of problems right now. Mr. Adolph told us that her mother moved away a few months ago, and hasn't seen the girls since."

"Her mom left?" Janelle asked.

"That's right. Mr. Adolph moved here so that he could start his own business and spend more time with his girls. So Katie is missing her mother, and missing her old house and school and friends. Sometimes when people brag and look for attention, it's because they feel unloved. Do you think that could be how Katie's feeling?"

Janelle shrugged. "I don't know," she said.

When Mrs. Wilson left Janelle closed her eyes and prayed. *Dear Jesus,* she prayed silently, *thanks for being with me today. Please help me get along with Katie. Help Katie be happier.* Janelle thought for a moment. *And please help her not brag so much. Otherwise she's going to drive me crazy.*

CHAPTER
5

As the Saddle Turns!

Janelle lay in bed Sunday morning, listening to the bustle in the kitchen. Her stomach growled as the smell of toast floated under the door. But Janelle wasn't ready to get up yet.

She thought about yesterday's Sabbath School class. Mrs. McFayden, her Sabbath School teacher, had read the story about the good Samaritan.

"A man was robbed and left to die at the side of the road. Two men walked by and ignored the hurt man. But the third man, a Samaritan, bandaged him, and took him to a safe place. Now, who was the hurt man's neighbor?" the teacher had asked.

Janelle knew that the Samaritan who had helped the hurt man was his real neighbor. Everyone knew that. *But am I acting like Katie's neighbor?* she wondered to herself.

Mrs. McFayden had said something that Janelle couldn't forget. "You can tell what a person believes by what they do."

At first Janelle hadn't really understood her, but the teacher had explained. "If you say you believe something in the Bible, but you don't do it, it shows you really *don't* believe it."

Katie closed her eyes. *Dear Jesus,* she prayed, *I believe that You want me to be kind to everyone. You want me to be like the good Samaritan. Help me be kind to Katie.* Janelle sighed. Katie was coming over this morning to ride again. *I don't know if I can be patient with her much longer. Please help me. Amen.*

Janelle felt a bit better as she swung her feet over the edge of the bed. *Now for something to eat,* she thought.

The air was already warm when Janelle went outside. Dozens of frogs peeped from a pond near her house, and the poplar trees were dressed in new, bright-green leaves. Janelle smiled. It was a beautiful spring day—how could anything go wrong?

At first it was easy to be patient with

Katie. Janelle let her help brush Prince, and didn't even mind when Katie insisted she could saddle Prince alone.

"I can do it," Katie had insisted. "I'm just as strong as you are."

Mr. Wilson watched as Katie rode the pony around the yard. "You're getting to be a real horse rider," he said.

Katie beamed. "Thanks," she said. "I like Prince, you know. And he sure does like me." The girl leant over and scratched the pony on the neck.

"But where's the riding helmet?" Mr. Wilson asked.

"It's too small," Katie said. "My head's bigger than Janelle's."

"Well, put it on anyway," Mr. Wilson said. "You never know when you're going to fall off."

"I won't fall off," Katie said, pouting. But she allowed Janelle to pass her the helmet, and buckled it under her chin.

"Say, Mr. Wilson," Katie called, after riding around the ring another time. "Can I take Prince down the lane? I'm getting tired of going around in circles."

Mr. Wilson hesitated. "I don't think so," he said slowly. "You've only been riding for a few weeks, Katie, and you may have problems making Prince obey."

"Janelle gets to ride alone," Katie said. Her voice was whiny now, and Janelle frowned. "And you just told me what a good rider I'm becoming."

Mr. Wilson scratched his head and thought for a moment. "Well," he said. "Here's the deal. You can ride Prince down the lane if Janelle will walk with you. That way Janelle can help if you have any problems."

"Great!" Katie beamed. Then she turned to Janelle. "Let's go," she ordered.

Janelle felt the smile slip from her face. She really didn't feel like walking up and down the lane with Katie. *My cowboy boots aren't very comfortable for walking,* Janelle thought. *Besides, it should be my turn now to ride.* Then she remembered her prayer that morning. "All right," she said with a sigh. "Let's go."

They were part way down the lane when Prince noticed a clump of tender grass. He came to an immediate halt, and put his head down to eat.

"Keep his head up," Janelle instructed.

"He just wants a few bites of grass," Katie said.

"I know," Janelle said impatiently. She took hold of Prince's bridle and pulled. "But he'll get spoiled if you let him eat during a ride."

"Boy, you're sure bossy," Katie said frowning.

Janelle pursed her lips together but didn't answer.

Now Katie looked mad. "Let go of Prince's bridle," she said sharply, trying to jerk the reins away from Janelle.

Janelle let go and stopped in the middle of the road. "Let's go back," she said.

"In a few minutes," Katie replied, kicking the pony's sides. Prince began to trot.

"You shouldn't trot here," Janelle said, watching as the pair moved away from her.

"Oh, stop telling me what to do," Katie snapped. "I can ride Prince as good as you can. Maybe better."

Janelle shrugged her shoulders. *Well, I tried to be nice, Jesus,* she thought with a frown. *But maybe You should tell Katie to be nice, too.* Janelle turned around and began walking back down the lane.

She was almost at the tack shed when the sound of running hooves made her turn around. There was Prince, galloping down the lane towards her! The pony's ears were flat against his head, and every few steps he bucked and kicked towards his belly. Katie was nowhere in sight!

As Prince raced closer, Janelle suddenly saw what had happened. Prince's saddle had slipped to the side, and was now swinging under the pony's belly. Stirrups and flaps of leather swung from side to side, frightening Prince. But where was Katie?

"Oh, no!" Janelle gasped as Prince ran past her, his eyes wild and frightened. Janelle wanted to catch him, but she had a bigger worry. Where was Katie? Had she been trampled under Prince? Janelle's heart pounded as she looked around frantically. What should she do?

Mr. Wilson appeared at the doorway of the garage.

"Dad!" Janelle screamed. "Something's happened to Katie!"

Mr. Wilson looked around the yard, and then seemed to realize what had happened. "Try to catch Prince," he called. "I'll take the car down the lane, and find Katie."

Janelle watched as Prince dashed wildly over to the corral and stood there, trembling. Janelle moved slowly towards him, calling his name. "Here, Princey boy," she coaxed softly. The pony tossed his head, but stood still.

"Come on, Princey boy," Janelle called. She held one hand towards the pony, and moved in slow, quiet steps.

Step by step, she approached Prince. Janelle could almost touch Prince when the little pony spun around on his hind legs. With every movement, the saddle flapped and slapped against the pony's legs.

"Whoa, Prince!" Janelle hollered. The pony didn't seem to hear her. He raced straight towards the barbwire fence near the corral.

There was a sickening *screech* as the pony hit the barbwire fence. The top wire snapped and Prince tumbled forward. He hit the ground with a *thud*, and then struggled to his feet. Prince stood still, trembling, as Janelle raced towards him.

In a moment, Janelle had her hands on the bridle. She took a firm grip, her own hands shaking. "What have you done, Princey boy?" she gasped.

A huge gash ran across Prince's chest, and drops of bright red blood trickled down his shoulder. Prince was hurt!

PRINCE

CHAPTER

6

Prince Is Hurt

Janelle and her mother managed to get the saddle off Prince without further problems.

"He's hurt pretty badly, isn't he?" Janelle asked, trying not to look at the terrible cut on Prince's chest.

Mrs. Wilson nodded. "I'm afraid so," she said. "It wouldn't surprise me if he needs stitches."

Janelle looked down the lane. "Where's Dad and Katie?" she asked. Janelle felt almost sick with worry. Prince was hurt. And what about Katie? Had she been dragged behind Prince? Was she trampled in the fall? Was she OK? It seemed to be forever before the Wilson car drove down the lane towards them.

When the car stopped Janelle rushed to the door and pulled it open. "Katie!" she exclaimed.

"Hi," Katie said with a weak smile. Her face and the black velvet riding helmet were covered with dirt. A stripe of red blood oozed from a cut under Katie's lip, and there was a hole in the elbow of her shirt.

"Are you OK?" Janelle asked.

Katie nodded. "I think so," she said.

Mr. Wilson got out of the car and looked at Prince. "Well," he said. "We'll need to have that cut checked. But first I'll take Katie back to her place."

"Is Prince hurt?" Katie asked, peering out the window.

"What do you think?" Janelle said sharply. "He did run through a barbwire fence!" *And it's all your fault,* she thought, frowning at Katie.

"Oh." Katie looked sad. She wiped her nose with a sleeve. "I hope he'll be OK."

"Me, too," Janelle said.

As Janelle started to shut the car door, Katie put out a hand. "Janelle," she said softly. "I'm sorry."

Janelle raised her eyebrows. "What?"

"I'm sorry," Katie repeated. "I'll never forgive myself for hurting Prince."

Janelle looked at Prince. *Saying sorry won't make Prince feel better,* she thought. The pony looked miserable. He stood quietly, with his head hung down. Even from the car, Janelle could see the bright red gash on his chest.

Angry words came to Janelle's mind, but she didn't know what to say. She didn't even know exactly how she felt. Anger and worry and frustration all swirled in her head. So Janelle didn't say anything.

In a minute, Mr. Wilson got into the car. "I'll be home as soon as I can," he said. "Phone the clinic and tell them we're bringing Prince in."

"Bye," Katie said.

Janelle raised one hand, and watched as the car drove down the lane. Then with a frown she turned to her pony. "I'll never forgive that Katie Adolph," Janelle said sharply as she looked at Prince.

Mrs. Wilson shook her head. "I know you're upset, honey," she said. "But never is a long time."

"Never," Janelle repeated. *And I don't care what You think, Jesus,* Janelle thought angrily. *It was Katie's fault.*

When Mr. Wilson returned from Katie's house he hooked the horse trailer onto the truck. They loaded Prince without any problems and started down the road.

"Maybe we should say a prayer," Mr. Wilson suggested as he turned the corner onto the main highway.

Janelle didn't answer. At this moment she didn't feel much like praying. But she listened as her parents prayed that the veterinarian would be able to help Prince. They also prayed that Jesus would be with Katie. Janelle felt a bit better at the end of the prayer.

"Did Katie say what happened?" Mrs. Wilson asked.

"Katie said that Prince was trying to go back home, and she was leaning in the saddle to try and turn him the other way. I guess she hadn't tightened the saddle snug enough, and it just slipped sideways. She fell underneath him, and hit her head on the hard road."

Janelle made a face.

"It's a good thing she was wearing Janelle's helmet," Mr. Wilson said. "And fortunately Prince didn't step on her."

"I'm glad she wasn't hurt worse," Mrs. Wilson said.

"Me, too," Mr. Wilson agreed.

Janelle nodded but didn't say anything.

In a few minutes, they stopped in front of the veterinarian clinic. "Poor Princey," Janelle said as they lead the pony into a large room in the back of the building. "He hates going to the doctor."

Dr. Tara, the lady veterinarian, remembered Prince from his visit last year. "Well, if it isn't my little doctor-hating pony," she laughed, patting Prince on the back. "Looks like you've got yourself into a real mess again."

Dr. Tara carefully examined the cut on Prince's shoulder. "I'm not going to be able to stitch this shut," she said, turning to the family. "The cut is just too wide—stitches won't hold."

"Will it get better?" Janelle asked. She almost felt sick looking at Prince's shoulder. Even now a small trickle of blood came from the cut.

Dr. Tara nodded. "I know it looks terrible," she said. "But if you care for the cut properly, I doubt it will even leave a scar. But it's going to take a lot of work, and you won't be able to ride Prince for a few weeks. Maybe longer."

"I'll help," Janelle said quickly.

"Good girl!" Dr. Tara said. "Now, here's what we need to do." The vet uncoiled a hose, and turned the water on slowly. "I want you to rinse Prince's cut with cold water twice a day. You'll need to hose him down for about five or ten minutes each time."

Prince jumped as the cold water hit his chest. The pony pranced around in the small place for a moment, and then seemed to realize that he wasn't being hurt.

"Cold water is actually very soothing," Dr. Tara explained. "It will help control the pain. And it stimulates growth of tissue, so the cut will heal quicker. And it will help keep the cut clean so infection doesn't start."

As Janelle watched, the pony let out a sigh and lowered his head. He stood quietly as Dr. Tara hosed off the cut. When she was finished, she took out an aerosol bottle, and sprayed some strong-smelling purple stuff on the cut.

"You'll need to apply this once a day," Dr. Tara said. "Now, we'll give Prince a shot of antibiotics, to make sure he doesn't get infection, and then he can go."

Prince seemed happy to be home. Janelle

threw the pony some hay and watched as he limped over to it, and began to eat slowly.

"We've got a lot of work ahead of us," Mrs. Wilson said.

"I know," Mr. Wilson agreed. "And I'm not going to be able to help you very much."

"I'll help," Janelle said. She dreaded the thought of looking at Prince's cut every day, but she was willing to do whatever it took to get her pony better.

"Well, tomorrow morning we'll have to get up early, before I go to work, and you go to school," Mrs. Wilson said, looking at Janelle.

"How early?" Janelle asked.

"We better give ourselves an extra half hour," Mrs. Wilson said with a sigh.

"Half an hour!?"

"Well, we have to catch Prince, and lead him over to the water tap, and rinse his leg for ten minutes. Then we spray it, and lead him back to the corral," Mrs. Wilson explained. "That's not going to be done in less than half an hour."

Janelle flopped back in the truck seat. She was tired, and angry, and sad. *This is all Katie's fault,* she thought. *I hope I never see her again.*

CHAPTER

Taking Care of Prince

Janelle's bedroom was still dark when her mother knocked on the door. "Time to get up," Mrs. Wilson called.

Janelle rolled over in bed and groaned. It was only 6:00 in the morning!

"And dress warmly," her mother called from the kitchen. "It's cool outside this morning."

This isn't cool, Janelle thought as they walked towards the corral. *This is cold— very cold!* White frost covered the grass, making it slippery under her rubber boots. Janelle pulled her coat collar up and shivered.

Prince was lying down in the corral. He

didn't get up until Janelle slipped the halter over his head and tugged lightly on the lead rope. Then with a groan he climbed stiffly to his feet.

"Poor Princey," Janelle said. For a moment she forgot her cold feet and hands. Prince's cut looked worse than ever. Dried blood crusted the dark hairs around the cut, and the whole shoulder looked swollen and painful. Prince limped as he followed Janelle out of the corral and over to the water tap.

Mrs. Wilson turned on the tap, and then helped Janelle hose down Prince's cut. The pony flinched when the water hit his shoulder, and for a few minutes they had problems making him stand still.

"Quit it, Prince!" Janelle scolded. "I'm getting more water on me than I am on you!"

Prince finally seemed to realize that the water wasn't hurting him, and stood quietly.

"That's ten minutes," Mrs. Wilson called, turning off the tap.

Janelle shivered. "We should dry Prince's leg," she said. "Otherwise he's going to be really cold."

"That's a good idea," Mrs. Wilson agreed. "Why don't you run into the house, and get one of our old towels? I'll lead Prince back to the corral."

After drying Prince, Janelle hurried back to the house. Her pants and socks were wet, so she changed into different clothes and ate a quick breakfast. Mrs. Wilson changed quickly so she could drive Janelle to school before going to work herself.

"This is going to be awful," Janelle moaned, as she grabbed her lunch bag and books. They were going to be late. "Do we really have to do this every morning?"

Mrs. Wilson didn't look very happy herself, but she nodded.

That's how the week passed. The mornings were the worst—rushing in the cold to wash Prince's leg and feed him before going to school. And then every evening going back to the corral, and doing the same thing all over again.

"Do you think his cut is looking any better?" Janelle asked her father one evening as he came out to help.

Mr. Wilson hesitated. "It's improving," he said. "But it's still got a long way to go."

"Prince still limps," Janelle said, stroking the pony's soft neck.

"I'm sure he does," Mr. Wilson said. "That's

a deep cut, and it's certain to hurt for a long time."

"But is it going to get better?"

Mr. Wilson nodded. "Yes, Janelle. I think he'll be fine. But you aren't going to be riding for a long time yet."

"Poor Princey," Janelle said. *And poor me. Here I finally have a horse of my own, and I can't even ride him!* she thought, feeling sorry for herself. *And it's all Katie's fault.*

Mr. Wilson turned to look at Janelle. "You're supposed to have 4-H tomorrow evening," he said. "Do you want to go?"

"Prince can't go!" Janelle said, surprised.

"No, I know *he* can't," Mr. Wilson agreed. "But you could."

Janelle looked doubtful. "What would I do at 4-H without a horse?" she asked.

"You can learn a lot just watching the other kids," Mr. Wilson said.

Janelle sighed. "That sounds boring,"

"Well, it's up to you," Mr. Wilson said. "I can drive you there if you decide to go. But it's your decision. Maybe you'd rather stay home and do some fence-mending with me."

Janelle rolled her eyes. Even going to 4-H without Prince had to be better than repairing the fence.

4-H was more interesting than Janelle had expected.

"This month we're going to do some jumping," the 4-H leader told the group. "We're going to start by trotting and cantering over poles on the ground. You and your horses will learn how to adjust your strides to go over the poles. Then in a few weeks' time we'll start doing some small jumps."

One girl raised her hand. "My horse has never jumped before," she said nervously.

"That's OK," the leader said. "We won't be doing anything difficult. All horses can jump a few inches, and some will jump much higher. This isn't a contest, it's just something we can work on to improve our riding control and skills." The leader reached over, and picked up a different looking saddle. "Does anyone here own an English saddle?" he asked.

An older girl at the back of the group raised her hand.

"Anyone who is interested can try riding English tonight," he said. "If you will notice, the English saddle does not have a horn, like your Western one's do. That makes it easier to jump."

"Why?" Janelle asked.

"Because the rider needs to lean forward when going over a jump," the leader explained. "When you lean forward in a Western saddle, the horn pokes you in the stomach."

The leader explained how the English saddle worked, and demonstrated it on his own horse. Janelle watched with interest.

"I'd like to try that," she whispered to her father.

He looked doubtful. "I think Prince is too short to be a good jumper," he said.

"Prince can jump great," Janelle said.

Mr. Wilson looked at his daughter. "What makes you so sure?" he asked.

"Don't you remember, Dad?" Janelle asked, trying not to smile. "What happened the very first time we saw Prince?"

Mr. Wilson began to smile. "Hmmm," he said, his lip twitching. "Now I remember."

"You and Uncle Brian were trying to catch Prince, and he jumped right over Uncle Brian's fence!" Janelle said. "Any pony that can jump that high—and that fast—should be able to go over those little jumps with his eyes closed!"

Mr. Wilson shook his head. "Well, honey," he said. "You've got a point. But it's going to be a while yet before you can ride Prince."

On the way home Janelle turned to face the side window and closed her eyes. She had hardly prayed all week, but suddenly she needed to. *Dear Jesus,* she prayed, *I think jumping would be so much fun. Please help Prince get better quickly.* She sat quietly for a moment, thinking. *And Jesus, please help Prince's leg not hurt anymore. That's more important than jumping, isn't it?*

She knew she should also pray for Katie. Didn't the Bible tell her to love her neighbor? And wasn't Katie her neighbor? But how could she pray for the person who hurt her pony? Especially when that person was bossy and annoying and a pest. Especially when the person was Katie Adolph.

Janelle sighed and closed her eyes. It was hard to know what to do. Part of her wanted to be mad at Katie—to punish her for hurting Prince. *But,* she admitted to herself, *I miss Katie. It was fun having someone to ride with. Even if things weren't perfect.*

Jesus, I'd like to forgive Katie, Janelle prayed. *But I can't seem to do it. You're going to have to help me. And Jesus, please forgive me for being so mad at Katie. Amen.*

CHAPTER

8

Not a Christian Pony

Katie phoned that evening.

You didn't have to answer my prayer that quickly, Jesus, Janelle thought with a small smile as she recognized the voice on the phone.

"How's Prince?" Katie asked. Her voice was small, as though she was far away.

"I still can't ride him," Janelle said. She wanted to say more—to let Katie know just how angry she was—but something about Katie's voice made her hesitate. Yes, Janelle was sad about her pony, but she could tell that Katie was sad too.

It was an accident, a small voice seemed to whisper in her ear.

Janelle remembered her prayer earlier, on the way home from 4-H. *Help me forgive Katie,* she had prayed. It had sounded impossible, but now as she listened to Katie, things seemed different. Prince was going to be OK. Maybe she should just forget being mad. It wasn't helping things, anyhow.

"Why don't you come over and see Prince?" Janelle asked suddenly.

There was a pause on the phone.

"Could I?" Katie asked.

"Sure," Janelle said. "I think he misses you."

"Does he?" Katie's voice was louder now. "I miss him too." The phone was quiet for a moment. "And I miss you too," Katie said.

The lump in Janelle's heart softened. How could she have been so mad at Katie?

"Come over tomorrow, after school," Janelle suggested. "And bring your rubber boots."

"My rubber boots?"

"You'll need them," Janelle said. "Wait and see."

Janelle smiled to herself after she hung up. *Thanks, Jesus,* she thought. *Being kind feels good.*

Janelle was rinsing off Prince's leg when

the Adolph car drove down the lane. Katie jumped out of the car, her brown ponytail bobbing, and waved goodbye to her father.

"I'll come back in an hour or so," Mr. Adolph called.

When Prince saw Katie he tossed his head and let out a soft nicker.

"Prince!" Katie exclaimed. She reached out to hug the pony's neck, and then stopped. "Oh, no!" she gasped. "Look at Prince's neck!"

Janelle looked at the pony. The cut was still deep, but it was definitely better than before.

"It's improving," Janelle said. "In fact, he's hardly limping anymore."

Katie didn't answer. Janelle saw the girl's eyes were full of tears. Both girls were quiet for a moment.

Then Prince shoved his nose towards them, asking them to scratch his head.

Janelle rubbed the pony's forehead. He pushed back, almost tipping the girl over.

"Prince, you silly thing!" Janelle laughed.

Katie didn't smile.

"I'm all done washing Prince's shoulder," Janelle said. "Let's take Prince for a walk down the lane. Dad said he needed some exercise."

"OK."

The pair started down the lane. Janelle walked on the pony's left side, leading him, and Katie walked on the other side. The only sound was the clip-clop of hooves on the hard road and the occasional chirp and twitter of the birds.

Just then a robin flew by with something black in its beak. Janelle pointed. "Did you see that?" she asked.

"What?" Katie asked.

"That bird."

Katie shook her head. "What about it?"

"It was carrying something in its beak. And do you know what it was?"

"No," Katie answered.

"Some of Prince's mane," Janelle said with a smile.

"What?"

"That's right," Janelle explained. "My dad and I trimmed Prince's mane a bit, and ever since then the birds have been hauling the long hairs off, and making them into nests. Isn't that funny!"

Katie began to smile. "I thought Prince looked different," she said. She reached out one hand and lightly touched the pony's neck.

"He's going to be OK, you know," Janelle said. "In fact, Dad said I could start riding him next week, if things go well."

"Aren't you mad at me?" Katie asked. "I mean, I'd have been mad if Prince was my pony and you hurt him."

Janelle paused. "Well," she said truthfully. "I was pretty angry at first."

Katie nodded. "I bet you were," she said. "So how come you're not mad now?"

Janelle stopped and let Prince graze on a patch of tasty grass at the edge of the road. "Well," she said. "It's a long story. And I don't want you to laugh at me."

"I won't laugh—honest!" Katie said quickly.

Janelle cleared her throat. "Well, you know I'm a Christian. And Christians are supposed to behave like Jesus."

"Uh-huh," Katie said, nodding her head.

"So the Bible says that Christians are supposed to forgive people, and treat them the way Jesus would. I knew Jesus wouldn't have stayed mad at you, so I prayed, and asked Him to help me forgive you. And somehow I just didn't feel mad anymore."

Katie raised her eyebrows. "Did you see an angel?" she asked.

Janelle laughed. "No," she said.

"So how do you know it was Jesus that helped you?" Katie asked. She scratched Prince's neck thoughtfully.

"I don't really know," Janelle said. "I just prayed about it, and Jesus seemed to solve the problem. I just wasn't angry anymore."

"That's neat," Katie said. "I'm glad you aren't mad. I've missed you a lot."

Just then Prince took another step forward to bite a delicious looking patch of grass. The girls had been so busy talking they hadn't noticed where the pony's hard, black hooves were.

Katie let out a loud shriek as the pony set his foot down—right on top of her rubber boot!

"Get off!" Katie yelled.

Janelle looked up, startled. There was Prince with his hoof standing right on top of Katie's toes.

"Get off, Prince!" Katie yelled again. She pushed against the black pony.

Prince looked at her curiously. He seemed to be wondering what all the noise and yelling was about. But he didn't move his feet.

Janelle grabbed hold of the lead rope and

tugged firmly. Prince planted his feet and pulled back.

"Get off, Prince!" Janelle yelled. She jerked even harder on the rope.

Finally with a sigh, the pony took a step forward. His foot came off Katie's. With a moan Katie bent over and rubbed her foot.

"Ouch, ouch, ouch," Katie groaned. "That really hurt."

She moaned for a moment and sank down to sit on the edge of the road. Katie pulled off the rubber boot and examined her foot. "Look! The top of my foot's all red now."

Prince ignored her, and began to eat again.

"Do you think it's broken?" Janelle asked.

Katie wiggled her toes. "I don't think so," she said. "But it sure hurts."

Katie held the one boot and began to walk back down the lane. Janelle tried not to smile, but Katie *did* look rather funny with one boot on and one boot off.

"Now you're both limping," Janelle said, looking at Katie and Prince.

"I think he did that on purpose," Katie said. She made a face at the pony. "You just wanted to hurt me because I let you get hurt!"

Prince swished his tail cheerfully. Janelle

looked at the sassy little face and bright brown eyes. *Ponies are smart,* she thought with a smile. *Maybe Prince did do it on purpose.*

"He's not acting very much like a Christian pony, is he?" Janelle said.

Katie giggled. "Yeah, you're right," she said. "Maybe you should take him to church next weekend."

"Maybe I should," Janelle agreed. "Maybe I should."

CHAPTER
9

Jump!

"Have a good ride," Mr. Wilson said as he passed the reins up to Janelle. "And make sure you don't work Prince too hard. The vet wanted him to take it easy this week."

Janelle rubbed Prince's neck. "Don't worry, Dad," she said. "We're just going to ride around the pasture."

Mr. Wilson turned to look at Katie, who was perched on the edge of her bike. "And you, young lady," he said. "Keep your bicycle helmet on when you ride. Especially when you're riding Prince. OK?"

"Yes, Mr. Wilson," Katie said meekly.

Janelle squeezed her legs, starting Prince down the narrow trail in the pasture. The pony glanced once or twice at Katie as she rode her bicycle on the path beside him.

"Is Prince scared of my bike?" Katie asked, pedaling easily.

"No," Janelle laughed. "Prince isn't scared of anything."

"Except birds," Katie said.

"And upside-down saddles," Janelle agreed. "But he isn't scared of bikes."

It felt wonderful to be back riding Prince. The little pony seemed to enjoy it too. He trotted merrily down the path, his black mane bobbing with every stride.

"He's not limping," Janelle called.

Katie smiled back at her.

When they had reached the far side of the pasture the pair stopped. Janelle dismounted from Prince, and held him while Katie climbed in the saddle.

"Are you sure the saddle's tight enough?" Katie asked, patting Prince's neck.

"It's good," Janelle said. "I checked it again."

Janelle climbed on Katie's bike and rode beside her friend. Katie kept the pony to a walk as the path curved around a clump of trees.

"Look," Janelle said, pointing to a bush

across from them. "There's going to be a lot of saskatoons this year."

"Where?" Katie asked.

Janelle stopped the bike by a tall bush, and pointed to the green clusters of berries. "See," she said. "I love saskatoons. But it's going to be a long time before they ripen."

"My mom used to make the best saskatoon pie," Katie said. She opened her mouth to say something else, and then closed it. They were quiet for a moment.

"You must miss your mom," Janelle said softly.

Katie nodded but didn't answer.

"We've been praying for you and your dad," Janelle said. She bent over and plucked a Brown-eyed Susan flower and twirled it in her hands.

"Thanks," Katie said softly.

A yellow butterfly flitted by and landed on the saskatoon bush. Both girls watched for a moment. Even Prince seemed to be enjoying the scenery.

"Well, let's keep going," Janelle said. She pushed with one foot and started the bicycle rolling down the path.

In a few minutes the two paths narrowed and joined into one. Tall trees hugged both sides of the trail, making a pleasant and shady place to ride. Janelle, on the bike, led the way, and Katie on Prince followed slowly. They had only gone a short distance when Janelle stopped.

"Watch out," Janelle called. "There's a fallen tree in the way here."

Janelle got off the bike and bent over to pick up the log that lay across the path. Suddenly she stood up and smiled.

"Hey, I've got an idea," Janelle said. "I'm going to make Prince jump over this!"

"Won't it hurt him?" Katie asked. "Your dad said to ride Prince slowly."

"This isn't very high," Janelle said. "Look, it's not even as tall as my knees. Hop off, OK?"

Katie pulled the bike out of the way and watched as Janelle mounted Prince.

"We can do it, Princey boy," Janelle whispered. She circled the pony away from the log, and then turned him to face it.

Prince trotted briskly up to the fallen tree, his ears pricked forward curiously. Janelle leaned forward a bit and loosened the reins.

Prince picked that second to slam on the brakes. The pony skidded to a stop in front of the log. Janelle continued forward. Her body slumped onto the pony's neck, and she would have fallen if she hadn't managed to grab hold of a thick handful of mane at the last moment.

"Are you OK?" Katie asked anxiously.

"I'm fine," Janelle said. "Now, if Prince wasn't such a big chicken!" She tried to ignore the way her heart was pounding in her chest.

Janelle rode the pony away from the branch again. This time she made him trot even faster towards the log. But Prince spooked long before they got there. He snorted and pranced sideways.

I hope I don't fall off, Janelle thought. But she gritted her teeth and turned Prince around sharply. She took Prince away from the log and then turned him in a straight line towards it. Then Janelle stopped the pony and patted his neck. She waited until he seemed more relaxed, and then ordered Prince into a brisk trot again.

Prince hesitated when the log was directly in front of them. Janelle brought her heels down firmly on the pony's sides and clicked her tongue. Prince paused—and then with a sudden jump, sprang over the little log. He jumped high and cleared the log with inches to spare.

Katie clapped excitedly. "You did it!" she cheered.

Janelle patted Prince's shoulder. "Good boy," she said. "That wasn't so hard, was it?"

Janelle then made the pony jump over the log from the other direction. This time he didn't hesitate, but bounced easily over the branches.

"I knew Prince would be a good jumper," Janelle beamed.

"That looks like fun," Katie said. "Can I try?"

Janelle shook her head. "Sorry," she said. "But I don't think you're ready to jump yet."

Katie frowned. "But—" she began.

Janelle stopped her. "No, Katie," she repeated.

Katie's voice took on a whiny tone. "How come you get to do all the exciting things and I have to make Prince walk all the time? It's not fair."

"It is fair," Janelle said firmly. "Katie, you're my friend. But I can't let you do something that wouldn't be safe for you or Prince."

"But—"

"No," Janelle said.

Katie sighed and picked up her bike. She wheeled the bike past the log, and then swung her leg over the bar. She began to pedal down the path, with Janelle and Prince following close behind.

The girls were quiet for a few minutes, and then Katie turned to Janelle. "Do you think I could jump Prince in the riding ring at home? I'd really like to try."

Janelle smiled at Katie. "We'll ask my dad and see what he says."

Katie nodded her head. "OK," she said.

Janelle began to hum as they trotted down the path. Then she suddenly broke into song. "I am so glad that Jesus loves me, Jesus loves me, Jesus loves me," she sang. "I am so glad that Jesus loves me, Jesus loves even me."

Janelle felt very happy. It was a beautiful day—Prince was almost all better. They had jumped a few times, and done well. And Katie was her friend again. What more could a girl want?

Thank You, Jesus, Janelle thought with a smile, glancing over at Katie. *Thanks for Katie and Prince and all the great things You've made. Help me be a good horse rider, and especially help me be a good friend.*

Janelle began to sing again. "I am so glad that Jesus loves me, Jesus loves even me."

CHAPTER
10

The Canada Day Parade

"The water's still too cold," Janelle called to her mother.

Mrs. Wilson adjusted the tap. "How's that?" she called.

"Better," Janelle said.

She began to run warm tap water over Prince's back. The pony pinned his ears back, but didn't move.

"Are you ready for the shampoo?" Katie asked.

"In a minute," Janelle said. Once Prince was totally wet, the two girls began to rub shampoo on him.

"I'm getting soaked," Katie grumbled, looking at her shirt.

"Now you know why we don't bathe Prince very often," Janelle said. She scrubbed Prince's mane firmly. "At least he's not scared this time. Last year when we bathed him, he was so nervous we could hardly hold him still."

"Well," Mrs. Wilson said. "Prince has seen a lot of water this summer, hasn't he? He shouldn't be scared of it anymore."

Janelle looked at the pony's shoulder. The wire cut was now healed, and all that remained was a small dimple on his shoulder.

"You have to look nice for the Canada Day Parade tomorrow," Janelle told Prince. She watched as muddy water trickled off the pony.

"I never knew Prince was so dirty," Katie said.

"That's one of the good things about a black pony," Janelle agreed. "They don't show the mud."

It took a long time to rinse all the bubbles off Prince, but finally they were satisfied.

Each girl then grabbed a curry comb. Janelle began to untangle knots in the pony's long tail while Katie worked on his mane.

"We should braid Prince's mane for the parade," Katie suggested.

"That's a great idea!" Janelle agreed.

In half an hour, Prince stood before them. He was damp, but clean. His hooves sparkled, and dozens of narrow braids lined the pony's neck. Each braid was tied with a bright red bow. Prince shook his head impatiently, making the braids jump and dance on his neck.

"OK, Princey boy," Janelle said, giving his shoulder one final pat. "I guess we better put you in the barn."

"Does he have to stay in the barn all night?" Katie asked.

"I'm afraid so," Janelle said.

"Why?"

"If we don't keep him in, he'll roll. And then all our hard work will be wasted," Janelle explained. She led the pony to the small barn, and put him inside the stall. Prince sniffed the fresh straw on the floor of the stall

They admired Prince for a few moments, and then Katie looked at her watch. "I guess I'd better phone my dad," she said. "I want to finish decorating my bike before it gets dark."

"Do you want me to help?" Janelle asked.

Katie shook her head. "No way," she said. "I want to surprise you at the parade tomorrow."

The girls smiled at each other.

July 1 was a beautiful, sunny day. Janelle couldn't help feeling a bit nervous as she packed her saddle and new red saddle blanket. She had never ridden in a parade before. She hoped that the noisy bands and the fluttering floats wouldn't scare Prince.

"You're not scared of anything, are you, Prince?" she whispered to the pony, hoping that it was true.

Help Prince be good, she prayed quickly. *Thanks, Jesus. Amen.*

Janelle's 4-H group was meeting near the local schoolyard. Dozens of horses stood quietly as children got ready to ride.

"I'll saddle Prince," Mr. Wilson offered. "But you need to check his mane."

Janelle looked at the pony's braided mane and then groaned. "Prince!" she said. "What have you done?"

Almost half of the pretty braids had been rubbed loose in the horse trailer that morning!

"You just *had* to scratch your neck, didn't you?" Janelle moaned.

"Should we fix them, or do you want to take all the braids out?" Janelle's mother asked.

"I want to fix them," Janelle said with a sigh. "But I didn't bring the red yarn."

Mrs. Wilson reached into her purse and held up the ball of yarn. "Is this what you're looking for?" she asked.

Janelle smiled broadly. "Thanks, Mom!" she said. Then she quickly began to re-braid the pony's mane. Mrs. Wilson cut several new lengths of yarn, and then began to braid a different section of mane. Before long they were finished.

Janelle stood back to admire her pony. He looked wonderful! His black coat shone and sparkled in the sunshine. The braids with their red bows danced on the pony's neck with every movement.

"I love my new saddle blanket," Janelle said. She admired the red blanket, and then looked at her own matching red shirt. "We look perfect for Canada Day," she said. "We even match the flag!"

"Speaking of flags," Mr. Wilson said. "Your leader has just called everyone. He's going to pass the flags to the bigger kids now, and then you'll be ready to head to the parade line."

The 4-H leader waved his hand. "Mark, Lisa," he called. "You're two of our older children. Can you ride over here, and I'll give you each a flag to hold?" The leader held up two large flags, one with the red and white Canadian maple leaf, and one with the blue 4-H symbols.

A faint breeze made the flags flap and snap. Maybe that was what scared the horses. Neither of them would stand still, and when the leader attempted to walk their direction, the whole group of horses became nervous.

The older girl finally was able to hold the staff of the blue 4-H flag. Janelle watched as she spoke softly to her horse, and calmed him down. But there was no way the older boy could persuade his horse to let the flag within reach.

The leader tried several other children, but all without success. In the distance they could hear band music playing, and the leader began to appear a bit worried.

"We don't have much time left," he said. "But we need someone else to carry a flag. Is there anyone here who thinks their horse would cooperate?" He looked around at the older children.

Janelle hesitated. Prince had been ignoring the whole episode. But what would he do if the flag came closer?

"Dad," Janelle hissed. "Prince isn't scared of anything."

"Except birds," Mr. Wilson hissed back.

"I know, I know," Janelle groaned. "But do you think he'd be frightened of the flag?"

"Well, let's find out," Mr. Wilson said.

He walked over to the 4-H leader, and picked up the bright red and white Canadian flag.

Prince lifted his head and watched as the flag came towards them. He flared his nostrils, and then relaxed. Mr. Wilson carefully passed the large flag to Janelle.

Janelle was surprised how heavy the flag was. But Prince wasn't the least bit worried by the flapping material.

The parade was wonderful. Janelle and the older girl rode at the front of the 4-H group, holding their flags. *I think Prince is trotting in time to the music,* Janelle thought with a smile. Her hand ached from holding the heavy flag, and her face was getting tired from smiling all the time. But she was glad she had come, and she was glad that Prince was healthy enough to ride again.

Just then a girl on a strange looking bicycle rode past and waved. Janelle looked up, and then began to laugh.

It was Katie. She was dressed in western clothes and wore a cowboy hat. But it was her bicycle that really caught Janelle's eye! She had made a cardboard horse that totally covered the bike! Two wheels peeked through the bottom of the cardboard horse.

The bike horse was painted black, and it had a mane and tail of black yarn. As Katie turned the corner Janelle thought she got a glimpse of something red in the black mane. Why, Katie had even braided her pretend horse's mane and tied it with red bows!

Janelle's smile spread even wider across her face. *Thank You, Jesus, for loving me,* she thought happily. *And thank You for Prince. I'm so glad to have a pony of my own. And thank You for my friend, Katie. Amen.*

If you enjoyed this book, you'll enjoy these other books in the **Julius and Friends series**:

Julius, the Perfectly Pesky Pet Parrot
VeraLee Wiggins.
0-8163-1173-0. US$6.99, Cdn$10.49.

Julius Again!
VeraLee Wiggins.
0-8163-1239-7. US$6.99, Cdn$10.49.

Tina, the Really Rascally Red Fox
VeraLee Wiggins.
0-8163-1321-0. US$6.99, Cdn$10.49.

Skeeter, the Wildly Wacky Raccoon
VeraLee Wiggins.
0-8163-1388-1. US$6.99, Cdn$10.49.

Lucy, the Curiously Comical Cow
Corinne Vanderwerff.
0-8163-1582-5. US$6.99, Cdn$10.49.

Thor the Thunder Cat
VeraLee Wiggins.
0-8163-1703-8. US$6.99, Cdn$10.49.

Prince, the Persnickety Pony
Heather Grovet.
0-8163-1787-9. US$6.99, Cdn$10.49.